LEVEL GREEN BOOKS
for young readers

THE TREETOP BIRD FAMILY

BY LORETTA MAGDEN

Illustrations by J. M. Barringer

Loretta Magden

Published by Level Green Books for Young Readers
11 Level Green Road, Brooktondale, New York 14817

Copyright © 2007 by Loretta Magden
Book design by Michael Rider, Rider Design, Ithaca, New York.
The text for this book is set in Adobe Jenson. The illustrations are rendered in pencil and gouache.

ISBN: 978-0-9788771-0-1   CIP data for this book is available from the Library of Congress.

Additional copies of this book and other books by Loretta Magden can be ordered directly
from the publisher at www.LevelGreenBooks.com.

Printed in China.   10 9 8 7 6 5 4 3 2 1

THIS BOOK IS DEDICATED TO MY CHILDREN, DAVID AND HALLIE

who inspired me to write. They have brought me more joy and happiness

than they will ever know. My thanks to Laurel Guy who made

this book happen. And finally, to the love of my life, Herbie, who patiently

and with a twinkle in his eye listens to all my stories.

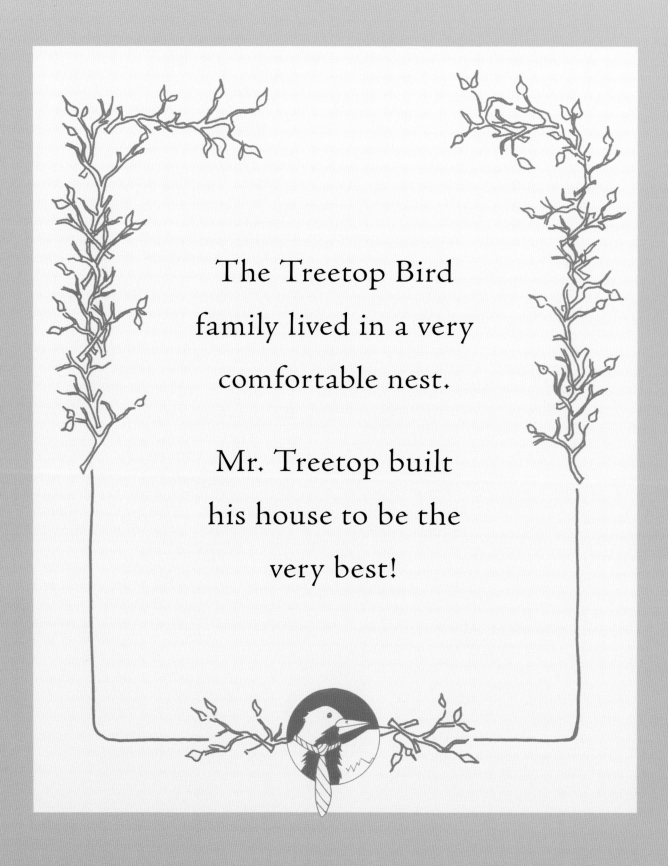

The Treetop Bird
family lived in a very
comfortable nest.

Mr. Treetop built
his house to be the
very best!

Mrs. Treetop wanted
to feed her children
a well-balanced diet.

But when she served
a nourishing 'worm'–
they wouldn't even try it!

They turned up their
beaks and only said,
"Yook! Yook! Yook!…

…that worm tastes
like the most awful
gook, gook, gook!"

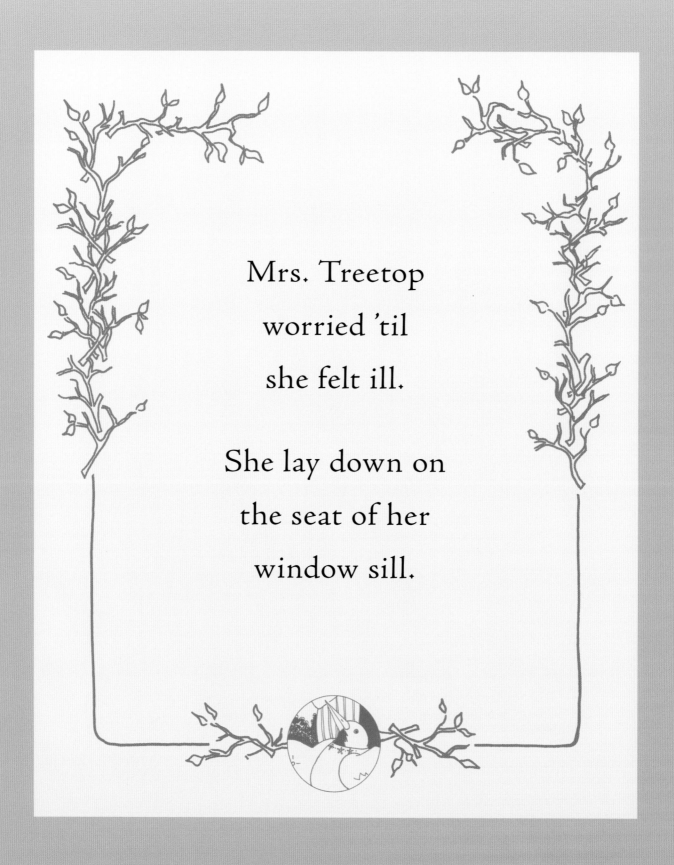

Mrs. Treetop
worried 'til
she felt ill.

She lay down on
the seat of her
window sill.

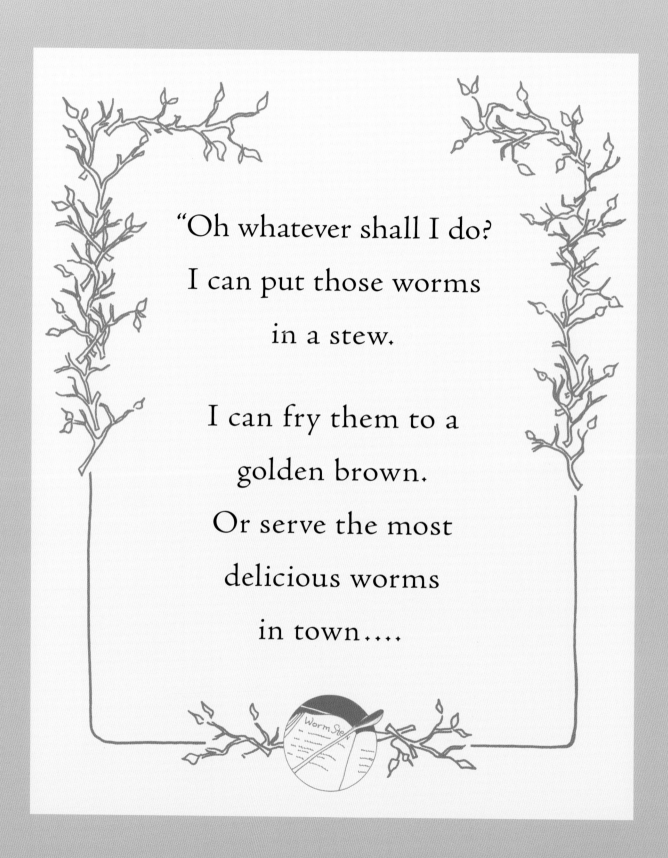

"Oh whatever shall I do?
I can put those worms
in a stew.

I can fry them to a
golden brown.
Or serve the most
delicious worms
in town....

The Joy
of
Worm
Cookery

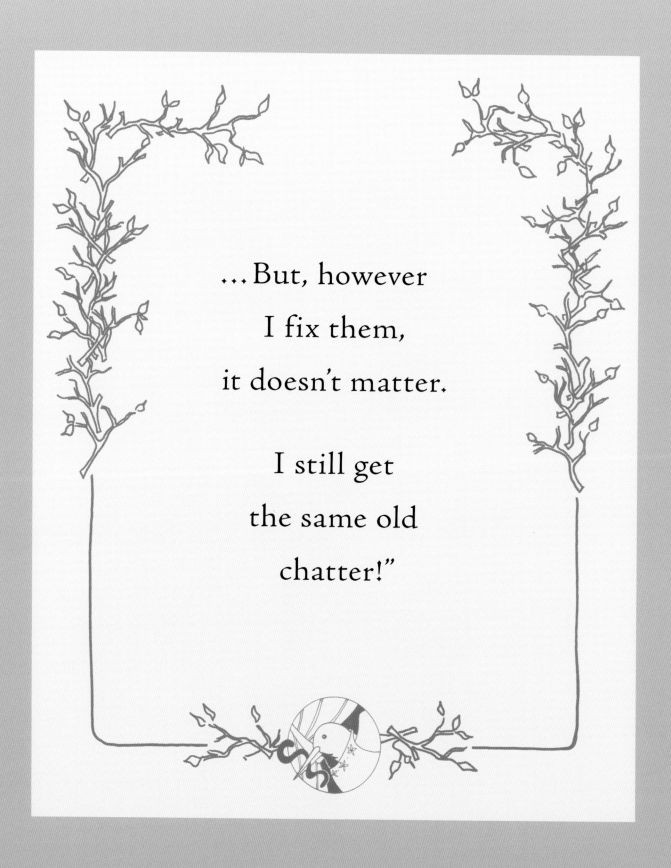

…But, however
I fix them,
it doesn't matter.

I still get
the same old
chatter!"

"Worms again!
Worms again!
Yook! Yook! Yook!

We are tired
of that awful
gook, gook, gook."

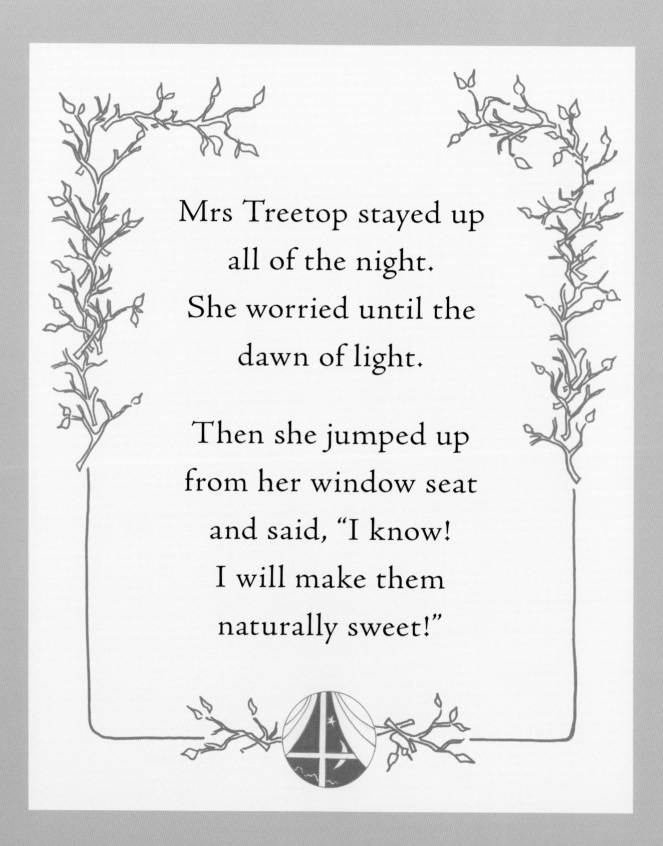

Mrs Treetop stayed up
all of the night.
She worried until the
dawn of light.

Then she jumped up
from her window seat
and said, "I know!
I will make them
naturally sweet!"

She mixed them
with honey, berries
and seeds.

Then baked them in

a pan of weeds.

She served that dish
for the evening dinner.

Her children smiled.
And ate.

She had a winner!

Broccoli Bird Nest Pie

Makes one 9-inch pie

CRUST: 2 cups packed, grated raw potato
½ tsp. salt
1 egg beaten
¼ cup grated onion
Heat oven to 400°

Set the freshly grated potato in a colander over a bowl. Salt it and leave it for 10 minutes. Squeeze out the excess water and add it to the remaining ingredients. Pat it into a well oiled 9 inch pie pan, building up the sides of the crust. Bake for 40–45 minutes until browned.

Turn oven down to 375°

FILLING: 1 heaping, packed cup grated cheddar cheese
1 large broccoli, broken into small flowerets
1 clove crushed garlic
¾ cup chopped onion
3 Tbs. olive oil
dash of thyme
½ tsp. basil
½ tsp. salt
2 eggs and ¼ cup milk beaten together
black pepper

Sauté onions and garlic, lightly salted, in olive oil for 5 minutes. Add herbs and broccoli and cook, covered, for 10 minutes, stirring occasionally. Spread half the cheese into the baked crust, then the sauté, then the rest of the cheese. Pour the custard over. Bake 35-40 minutes until it is set.

SWEET WORM KUGEL

TOPPING: 2 cups crushed corn flakes
               ½ cup sugar
               ¼ stick melted butter

Mix together all ingredients and set aside for later

KUGEL: 8 oz. package egg noodles
               ¾ stick melted butter
               3 oz. cream cheese
               ½ cup sugar
               3 beaten eggs
               1 cup milk
               1 cup apricot nectar

Cook noodles, drain. Toss noodles with melted butter and put into a greased pyrex dish (about 13"x 9"x 2").

Cream the cream cheese with sugar; then add beaten eggs and mix together. Add milk and apricot nectar. Pour over the noodles.

Put topping on top of noodle mixture. Bake at 350°F for ¾ hour and then leave in warm oven for 20 minutes.

POLLACK STUDIO

LORETTA MAGDEN has been writing poetry and children's stories for forty years. She first began writing for her own children and her vivid imagination, sense of humor and insight continue to inspire her work. Loretta resides in Beachwood, Ohio with her husband Herb, has two grown children and three grandchildren.

J. M. BARRINGER began her artistic career by drawing in the margins of standardized tests with a No. 2 pencil. Other media followed; from Crayolas to poster paints, on to a Rapidograph, and the final frontier, the computer. Having spent 25 years as a graphic designer, she has turned once again to a simpler way of life where Crayolas, gouache, and her old favorite, the No. 2 pencil, reign supreme.

LAUREL GUY